THE CHILDREN'S CLASSICS Collection

Volume 2

Dados Internacionais de Catalogação na Publicação (CIP) de acordo com ISBD

W671t Wilde, Oscar.
The Happy Prince and other stories / Oscar Wilde. - Jandira, SP : W. Books, 2025.
120 p. ; 12,80cm x 19,80cm - (Classics).

ISBN: 978-65-5294-115-2

1. Literatura inglesa. 2. Clássicos. 3. Aventura. 4. Fantasia. 5. Imaginação. I. Título.
II. Série.

2024-2495 CDD 823
CDU 821.111-31

Elaborada por Lucio Feitosa - CRB-8/8803
Índice para catálogo sistemático:
1. Literatura inglesa 823.
2. Literatura inglesa 821.111-31

Text based on the original story by Oscar Wilde,
adapted by Catherine Veitch
Illustrations by Archina Laezza

1st edition in 2025
www.cirandacultural.com.br

The Happy Prince

and Other Tales

Oscar Wilde

W. Books

The Happy Prince

Little Swallow

The giant

The little boy

Water Rat

Mother Duck

Green Linnet

Hans

The miller

The rocket

The Happy Prince

Chapter One

A statue of the Happy Prince stood in the city square on a tall column, high above the city. His metal body was covered with leaves of fine gold, he had two bright sapphires for eyes, and a large red ruby glowed at the top of his sword.

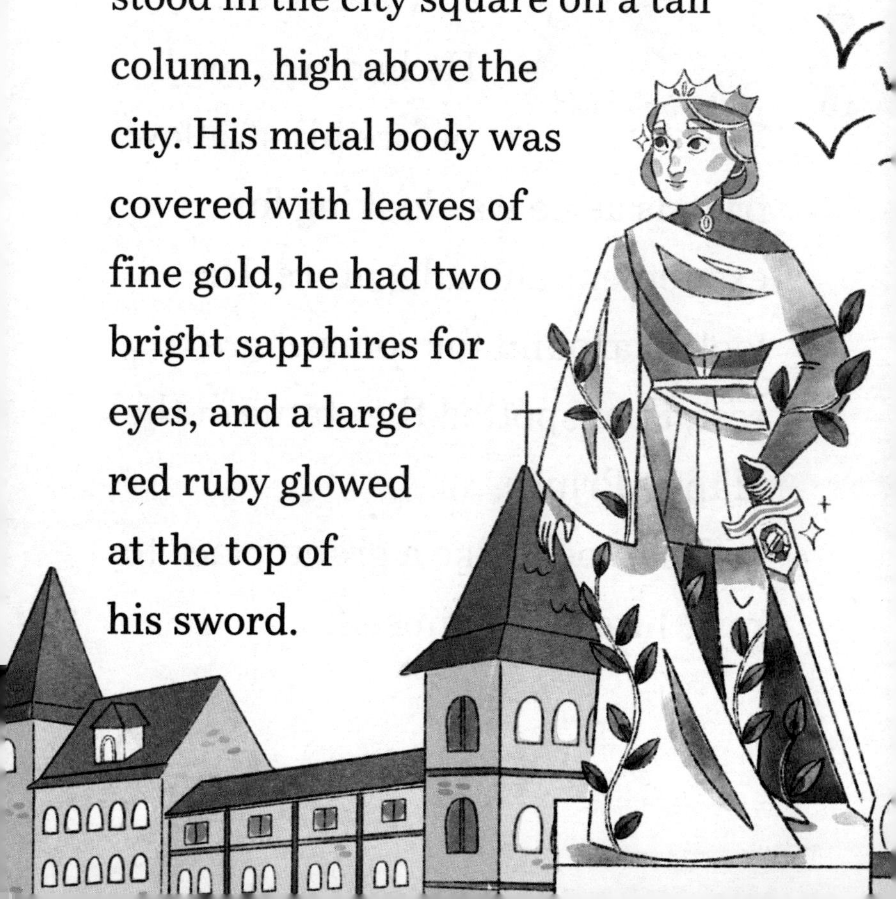

Everyone who lived in the city admired the Happy Prince.

One night a little swallow flew over the city. He had flown all the way from Egypt and was tired. He had returned before his swallow friends as he was looking for excitement and adventure. He looked around for somewhere to rest, then spotted the statue of the Happy Prince.

'That looks like a grand place to rest,' he said to himself.

He flew down and snuggled between the feet of the Happy Prince.

I have a golden bedroom! he thought, as he settled down to sleep.

But just as the swallow was tucking his head under his wing, a large drop of water fell on him. Then another drop fell. He thought it was strange that it was raining as there were no clouds in the sky – only bright, twinkling stars.

'What is the use of a statue if it cannot shelter me from the rain?' he muttered crossly. 'I will look for a good chimney pot instead.'

But before the swallow left, a third drop fell. He looked up. He was surprised to see the eyes of the Happy Prince were filled with tears, and more were running down his golden cheeks.

'Who are you?' the swallow asked the prince.

'I am the Happy Prince.'

'Why are you crying then?' questioned the swallow. 'You have soaked me!'

'When I was alive and had a human heart,' answered the statue, 'I did not know what tears were. I lived in a palace, where no one was unhappy. Every day I played with my friends in the garden, and every evening, I danced. There was a huge wall around the palace. I never asked what things were like on the other side of the wall. Everything about my life was beautiful. My courtiers called me the Happy Prince and I lived a long, happy life. When I died, they

courtiers

People from high-ranking families who spend a lot of time at the palace of a king or queen.

put me up here. Now I can see the city beyond the palace walls and I can see lots of sad things, which make me weep.'

The swallow looked at the Happy Prince. He was not sure what to say.

'Far away,' continued the statue, 'I can see a little house in a narrow street. One of the windows is open and there is a woman sat at a table inside. Her face is thin and worn, and she has rough, red hands that have needle pricks all over them as she is a seamstress. She is sewing flowers onto a satin gown for one of the queen's maids to wear at the next palace ball. Her little boy is ill in bed in a corner of the room. He has a fever and is asking for oranges. His mother has nothing to give him but dirty water, so he is crying.'

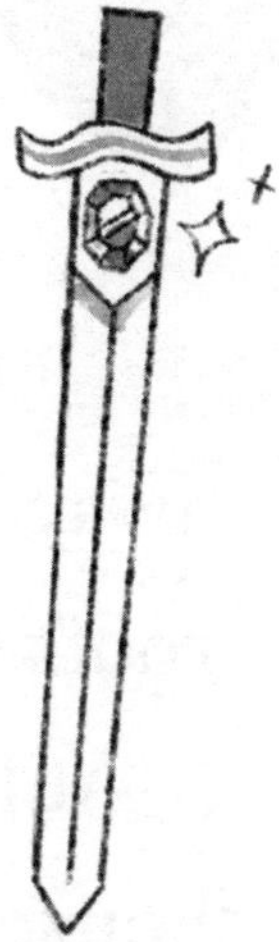

Suddenly, the Happy Prince had an idea. 'Little Swallow, can you take the ruby out of my sword handle and give it to the poor woman?' he asked, a glimmer of hope in his voice. 'My feet are fixed to this column and I cannot move.'

The swallow wanted to return to Egypt – it was too cold here – but the prince was so sad

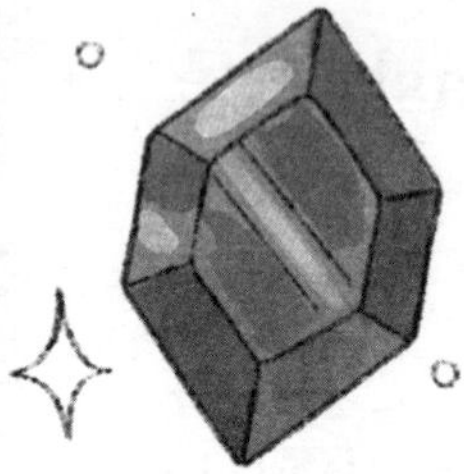

that the swallow agreed to help him first. He carefully pecked out the beautiful ruby from the prince's sword and flew away with it in his beak, over the roofs of the town.

At last he came to the little house the prince had described. The boy with a fever was tossing in his bed and his mother was so tired that she had fallen asleep. The swallow hopped in through the open window and laid the large ruby on the table beside the woman's thimble. Then he flew gently round the bed, fanning the boy's forehead with his wings. The boy started to feel cool and thought he must be getting better. Then he sank into a beautiful sleep.

The swallow flew back to the Happy Prince and told him what he had done.

Chapter Two

The next day, the swallow flew down to the river to have a bath.

'It is strange to see a swallow here in winter,' said a man who was passing over the bridge.

The swallow had made up his mind to return to Egypt that night. He spent the day sightseeing, flying around other important statues in the city, then he went to say goodbye to the prince.

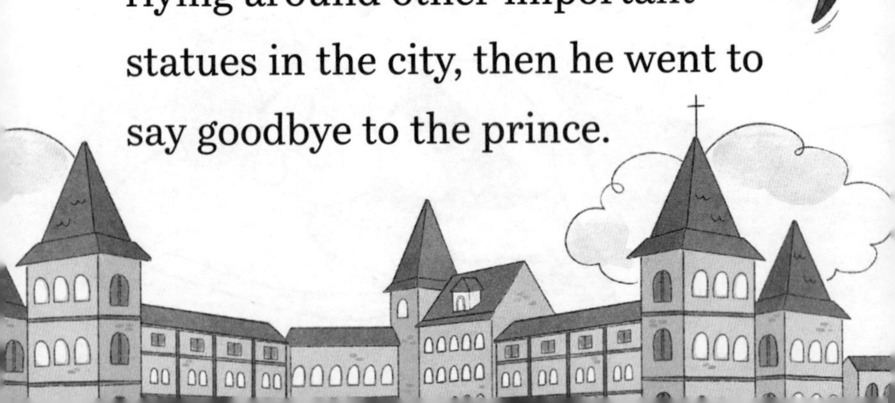

‘Little Swallow, can’t you stay with me for one more night?’ asked the prince.

‘My friends are waiting for me in Egypt. Besides, it’s too cold for me here,’ replied the swallow.

‘Little Swallow,’ said the prince pleadingly, ‘a long way across the city, I see a young man in an attic room. He is leaning over a desk covered with papers and by his side there’s a bunch of drooping violets in a little vase. He is trying to finish writing a play but he is

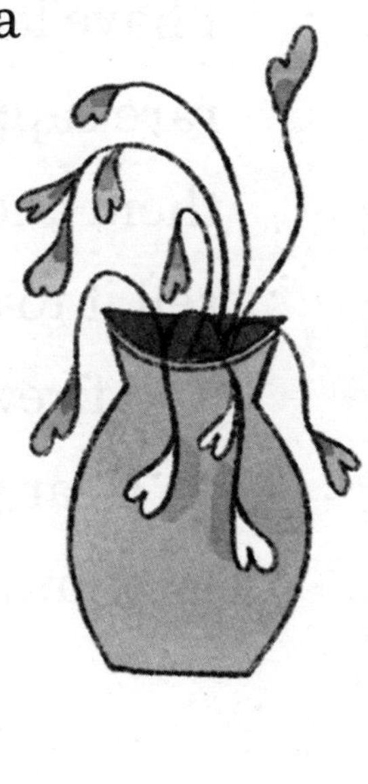

too cold to write any more. There is no fire in the fireplace. He is weak with hunger.'

'I will stay with you one more night,' said the swallow, who had a good heart. 'Shall I take another ruby to the man?'

'I have no more rubies,' said the prince. 'The only precious jewels I have left are my eyes. They are rare sapphires. Pluck out one of them and take it to him. He will sell it to a jeweller and buy food and firewood, and finish his play.'

'Dear prince,' replied the swallow, 'I cannot do that.'

'Do as I tell you, Little Swallow,' said the prince.

The swallow plucked out the prince's eye and flew away to the young man's attic room. It was easy to fly in as there was a hole in the roof. The young man had his head buried in his hands so he did not hear the flutter of the bird's

wings as the swallow quickly flew in and out again. When the man looked up, he found the beautiful sapphire lying next to the drooping violets. He looked at it, amazed.

'Now I can eat! And finish my play!' smiled the young man.

The next day the swallow flew down to the harbour. He sat on the mast of a large ship and watched the sailors heaving big chests onto the ship with ropes. 'Heave a-hoy!' they shouted as each chest went on.

The swallow wondered where they were sailing to, and if they might be going to Egypt.

Later that evening, he flew back to the Happy Prince.

'I have come to say goodbye,' he said sadly.

'Little Swallow, can't you stay with me for one more night?' asked the prince.

'It is winter here,' replied the swallow, 'and soon the snow will come, and there will be no food for me. In Egypt, the warm sun shines on the green palm trees. My friends are out there building their nests, waiting for me. Dear prince, I must leave you but I will never forget you. Next spring, I will bring you back two beautiful jewels in place of those you have given away. The ruby will be redder than a red rose, and the sapphire will be as blue as the sea.'

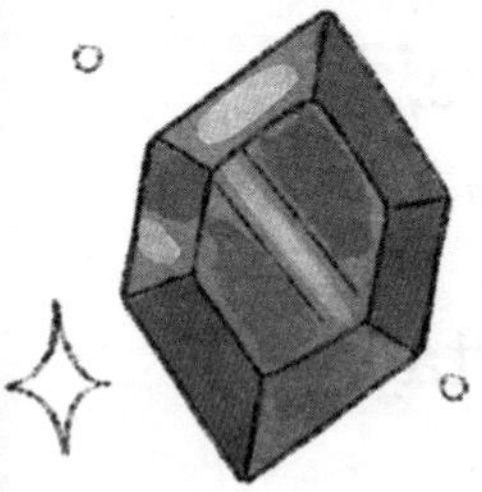

'But before you go, please do one last thing for me,' requested the Happy Prince. 'In the square below, there is a little girl selling hot spiced gingerbread. She has dropped her gingerbread on the ground and ruined it. Her parents will be angry with her if she does not bring home some money. She is crying. She has no shoes or tights and no hat on her little head. Pluck out my other eye and give it to her, so her parents will not be angry with her.'

'I will stay with you for one more night,' said the swallow, 'but I cannot pluck out your other eye, as then you would be blind.'

'Do as I tell you, Little Swallow,' said the prince.

So the swallow reluctantly plucked out the prince's other eye and flew down with it. He swooped past the little girl and dropped the jewel carefully into her hand.

'What a lovely bit of glass,' cried the little girl, and she ran home to show her parents.

Then the swallow went back to the prince.

'You cannot see now,' he said, 'so I will always stay with you.'

'No, Little Swallow,' replied the prince. 'It is too cold for you here. You must fly back to Egypt.'

'I will always stay with you,' said the swallow. He slept at the prince's feet.

Chapter Three

For the whole of the next day, the swallow sat on the prince's shoulder and told him stories of what he had seen on his travels – marvellous stories of things such as the tall birds called ibises, which stand in rows along the banks of the River Nile in Egypt and catch golden fish in their beaks.

'Dear Little Swallow,' said the prince after hearing the bird's tales, 'please fly over my city and tell me what you see there.'

So the swallow flew over the great city. He saw some people having fun in their beautiful houses whilst others sat outside in the cold. Under the archway of a bridge two little boys were lying in one another's arms to keep warm.

He flew back and told the prince what he had seen.

'I am covered with fine gold leaves,' said the prince. 'You must peck them off and give them to people in need.'

The swallow pecked off leaf after leaf of gold, until the Happy Prince looked dull and grey. He took the gold to the people who needed it. The children's faces grew rosier and they played games happily in the street.

'We can have bread now!' they cried.

Then the snow came, and after the snow came the frost. The streets sparkled as if they were made of silver. Long icicles hung down from buildings like sharp dinosaur teeth. People dressed in thick winter coats and woolly hats and gloves.

The poor little swallow grew colder and colder, but he would not leave the prince because he loved him so much. He picked up crumbs from outside the baker's door when the baker was not looking, and tried to keep himself warm by flapping his wings. He knew that he was going to die.

One day he was so weak, he had just enough strength to fly up to the prince's shoulder once more.

'Goodbye, dear prince!' he whispered.

'I am glad that you are going to Egypt at last, where you will be warm,' said the prince. 'You have stayed here too long.'

'I am not going to Egypt,' replied the swallow. 'I am leaving this world.'

And he kissed the Happy Prince on the cheek, and fell down dead.

At that moment there was a crack inside the statue, as if something had broken. The prince's metal heart had snapped in two.

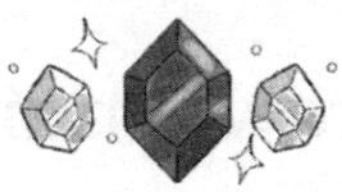

Early the next morning, the mayor was walking in the square. As he passed the column the Happy Prince's statue stood on, he looked up. He was shocked.

'The Happy Prince looks so tatty!' he exclaimed. 'The ruby has fallen out of his sword, his eyes are gone, and he is no longer golden. And there is a dead bird at his feet!'

The mayor ordered workmen to pull down the statue of the Happy Prince and to replace it with a statue of himself. The prince's statue was thrown into a furnace to melt it, so the metal could be made into something else.

But this was not the end of the prince. Something strange happened in the furnace. The prince's broken

furnace

An enclosed space in which a very hot fire is made to melt metal.

metal heart would not melt, so it was thrown away on a rubbish heap, where the dead swallow also lay. The Happy Prince and the swallow were together again, and they lived on happily ever after in the next life.

The Selfish Giant

Chapter One

Every afternoon, a group of children played in a giant's garden on the way home from school. The giant had been away visiting a friend for seven years, and the children didn't think the garden belonged to anyone.

It was a large garden with soft, green grass that had beautiful flowers sprinkled over it like stars. There were twelve peach trees, which had delicate pink blossom in the spring and rich fruit in the autumn. Birds sat on the trees and sang so sweetly that the children stopped playing so they could listen to them.

One day the giant came home and saw the children playing in his garden. Now he was back, he wanted the garden all to himself.

'What are you doing here?' he cried angrily. The children ran away. 'This is my garden,' said the giant. 'No one can play in it but me!'

The angry giant built a high wall all around his garden, and put up a sign:

Now the children had nowhere to play. They wandered around the high wall when their lessons were over, talking about the beautiful garden on the other side and how happy they had been playing in it.

Spring came. All over the country, blossom grew on trees and little birds sang. But it was still winter in the garden of the selfish giant.

The birds did not want to sing in it as there were no children, and the trees forgot to blossom. The snow and the frost were pleased that spring had forgotten the garden, as it meant they could stay there all year. The snow covered the grass with its huge, white blanket. The frost painted all the trees silver.

Then the cold north wind came. He blew over the garden all day and roared down the chimney pots on the giant's castle. Then the hail came. Every day he rattled on the castle roof until he broke most of the roof tiles, then he ran around the garden as fast as he could. He was dressed in grey and his breath was like ice.

'I cannot understand why spring is so late this year,' said the selfish giant to himself as he sat at the window and looked out onto his cold, white garden. 'I hope the weather will change soon.'

But spring, summer and autumn never came to the giant's garden. It was always winter there. The north wind, the hail, the frost and the snow danced around the trees all year round.

Chapter Two

One morning the giant was lying awake in bed when he heard some lovely music. It sounded so sweet that he thought it must be the king's musicians passing by. It was really only a little bird singing outside his window, but it was so long since he had heard birdsong in his garden that it sounded to him like the most beautiful music in the world. The hail stopped dancing on his roof and the north wind stopped roaring. Instead, a sweet scent wafted through an open window.

'I think spring has come at last!' cried the giant happily. He jumped out of bed and looked outside.

There he saw something wonderful. The children had crept into his garden through a small hole in the wall and they were sitting in the branches of the trees. On every branch, there was a little child!

The trees were so glad to have the children back again that they had covered themselves with blossom and were waving their branches gently above the children's heads. The birds were happy too and flew around twittering, as

the flowers poked their heads up
through the green grass, laughing.

'Now I know that it's the children who make my garden beautiful,' said the giant.

It was a lovely picture, but in the furthest corner of the garden it was still winter. A little boy was standing there. The boy was so small that he could not reach up to the branches of the tree to climb it and he was wandering around it, crying bitterly. The poor tree was still covered with frost and snow. The north wind blew and roared above it.

The giant's heart ached when he saw the boy. 'I have been so selfish,' he said. 'I will help that poor little boy up into the tree. Then I will knock down the wall and my garden will be the children's playground forever.'

He crept downstairs and went out into the garden. But when the children saw him, they were so frightened that they all ran away, and the garden became winter again. Only the little boy did not run, because his eyes were so full of tears that he did not see the giant coming.

The giant lifted the little boy gently in his hand and put him up in the tree. At once, the tree burst into blossom and the birds came and sang on it. The little boy flung his arms around the giant's neck and hugged him.

When the other children saw that the giant was not mean anymore, they ran back into the garden, bringing spring with them.

Chapter Three

'This is your garden now, little children,' said the giant.

He knocked down the wall with a huge hammer. The giant and the children played in the garden for the rest of the day. When it was time to say goodbye, the giant looked around for the little boy he had helped. He could not see him anywhere.

‘Where is the boy I put in the tree?’ the giant asked.

‘We don’t know. He has gone away,’ the children replied.

‘Tell him to come here tomorrow,’ said the giant.

But the children said that they did not know where the little boy lived and they had never seen him before. This made the giant sad.

Every afternoon, when school was over, the children came and played with the giant. But the little boy never came. The giant was very kind to all the children but he longed to see his first friend again.

Years went by and the giant grew old and frail. The children of the town still came to play in his garden. The giant could not run around with the children anymore so he sat in a huge armchair, looking out at his beautiful garden and watching the children play their games.

'I have many beautiful things in this garden,' he said, 'but the children are the most beautiful of all.'

One winter morning, the giant looked out of his window as he was dressing. He did not hate the winter now. He knew that spring was only asleep and the flowers were resting, and that they would soon come again.

Suddenly the giant saw something in the furthest corner of the garden. A tree was covered with lovely white blossom. Its branches were golden and silver fruit hung from them. Underneath the tree was the little boy who had been his first friend.

The Devoted Friend

Chapter One

One morning, old Water Rat put his head out of his hole. Little ducks swam in the pond. Their mother was trying to teach them how to stand on their heads in the water. Every now and then she showed them how it was done, but the little ducks were not listening.

'Such naughty children!' cried Water Rat.

'Nonsense,' replied Mother Duck.

'Everyone has to start somewhere. Parents need to be patient.'

'I don't know anything about how parents feel,' said Water Rat. 'I do not have any children. I have also never been married. I do have lots of friends, though. My friends are important to me.'

'What makes a good friend?' asked Green Linnet, who was

sitting in a willow tree nearby and had overheard them chatting.

'What a silly question!' cried Water Rat. 'I would expect my friends to do anything for me, of course.'

'What would you do in return?' asked a little bird, swinging on a water reed and flapping his tiny wings.

'I don't understand,' replied Water Rat.

'I will tell you a story that may help you,' said Green Linnet.

green linnet
Another name for a greenfinch, a small garden bird.

‘Is the story about me?’ asked Water Rat.

‘In a way,’ said Green Linnet, who flew down to rest on the bank. ‘Once upon a time …’

Once upon a time, there was an honest fellow called Hans. He lived in a tiny cottage all by himself, and every day he worked in his garden. There was no garden as lovely as his in all the countryside.

He grew beautiful flowers with unusual names, such as sweet William, gillyflower and shepherd's purse. There were also pink roses, yellow daffodils, lilac crocuses and purple violets.

Hans had many friends, but his best friend was the miller. The miller was rich as he earned lots of money from his mill. Every time the miller passed Hans's garden, he leant over the wall and plucked a large bunch of flowers or a handful of sweet herbs, or filled his pockets with plums and cherries if it was the right time of year for fruit.

'True friends share things,' the miller said. Hans nodded and smiled, and felt proud to have a friend who said such splendid things.

The neighbours, however, did not think so much of the miller. They thought it was strange that the rich miller never gave Hans anything in return. He had one hundred sacks of flour stored in his mill, six cows and a large flock of woolly sheep. But Hans never thought about that. He loved listening to all the wonderful things the miller said about what makes a true friend.

Chapter Two

Hans busily worked away in his garden all year. During the spring, summer and autumn he was happy, but when the winter came, his garden was bare. He had no fruit or flowers to sell at the market and did not make any money. He was cold and hungry, and often went to bed without any supper. He was also very lonely in the winter, as the miller never went to visit him then.

'I won't see Hans in the winter. When people are in trouble, they should be left alone and not bothered by visitors,' the miller said to his wife. 'When the spring comes, I will visit Hans again.

He will give me a large basket of primroses and that will make him happy.'

'You say such wonderful things,' said his wife, as she sat in her comfy armchair by a roaring fire.

'Can't we ask Hans to come here?' said the miller's youngest son. 'If poor Hans is in trouble, I will give him half my porridge. And I'd like to show him my white rabbits too.'

'Don't be silly, boy!' cried the miller. 'I wonder what things they teach you at school. If

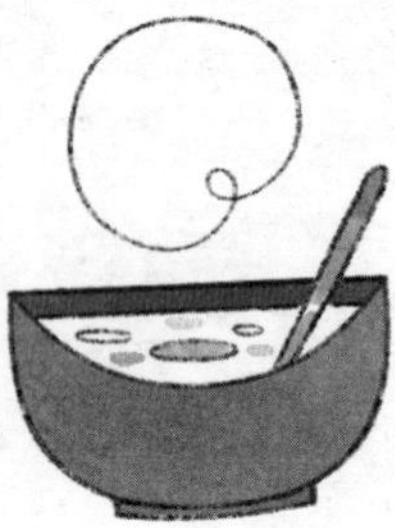

Hans came here and saw our warm fire and our tasty supper, he might get jealous. Jealousy is a terrible thing, which would turn Hans into a nasty person. I am Hans's best friend, and I will

not allow that to happen. Besides, if Hans came here, he might ask me to let him have some flour for free and I could not do that. Flour is one thing and friendship is another, and the two things should not be mixed.'

'How well you talk!' said the miller's wife, pouring herself a warm cup of tea.

'Lots of people do good things,' replied the miller, 'but many cannot talk as well as me. Talking well is much more difficult than doing good things, and it is much grander.'

The miller looked sternly across the table at his little son, who felt so ashamed of himself that he hung his head and blushed.

As soon as winter was over and the primroses began to open their pale yellow flowers, the miller said to his wife that he would go down to see Hans.

'You have such a good heart! You are always thinking of others,' cried his wife. 'Don't forget to take the big basket with you to fill with flowers.'

So the miller went down the hill with the basket on his arm.

'Good morning, Hans,' said the miller cheerfully when he got to his friend's house.

'Good morning,' said Hans, leaning on his spade and smiling from ear to ear.

'How have you been over the winter?' asked the miller.

'It's good of you to ask. I've had a hard time but now spring is here, I am happy, and all my flowers are doing well,' replied Hans.

'Your primroses are looking lovely,' said the miller.

'I am going to take them to the market and sell them. Then I will buy back my wheelbarrow with the money,' said Hans.

'Why did you sell your wheelbarrow? That is a silly thing to do!' said the miller.

'I had to,' replied Hans. 'The winter was so hard for me that I had no money to buy food. First, I sold the silver buttons off my Sunday coat, and then I sold my silver chain. After that I sold my big pipe. Lastly, I sold my wheelbarrow. But I am going to buy them all back again now.'

'My old wheelbarrow is broken – one side is gone and there is something wrong with the wheels – but I will give it to you. I know it is very generous of me, and many people will think I am silly for giving it away, but I am not like other people. I think that being generous is what makes a good friend. And I have bought a new wheelbarrow for myself, so I can give you my old one,' said the miller.

'Thank you. That is very generous of you,' said Hans, his round face shining with happiness. 'I can easily repair it as I have a plank of wood in the house.'

'A plank of wood is just what I want for the roof of my barn,' said the miller. 'There is a large hole in it, and all the corn will get damp if I don't cover it up. It's lucky you mentioned it! It is quite amazing how one good act always leads to another. I am going to give you my wheelbarrow, and now you are going to give me your plank. Of course, the wheelbarrow is worth far more than the plank, but true friends don't notice things like that. Get the wood at once! I will repair my barn today.'

'Of course,' cried Hans. He ran into the shed and came back with the plank on his shoulder.

'It is not a very big plank,' said the miller, looking at the wood.

'I am afraid that after I have mended my barn roof, there won't be any wood left for you to mend the wheelbarrow with, but that is not my fault. And as I am giving you my wheelbarrow, I am sure you would like to give me some primroses in return. Here is my basket. Make sure you fill it to the top.'

'To the top?' asked Hans, rather sadly. It was a very big basket and Hans knew that if he filled it to the top, he would have no primroses left to sell at the market. He had really wanted to buy his silver buttons back.

'As I am giving you my wheelbarrow, I don't think a few primroses is too much to ask for,' said the miller. 'I would have thought that real friends were not selfish like that.'

'My dear, best friend,' cried Hans, 'you are welcome to all the flowers in my garden. I would much rather you think good things of me than have my silver buttons back.'

Hans ran and plucked all of his

pretty primroses and filled the miller's basket.

'Goodbye, Hans,' said the miller, as he went up the hill with the plank on his shoulder and the big basket of primroses in his hand.

'Goodbye,' said Hans. He went back to happily digging in his garden. He was so pleased he was getting the miller's wheelbarrow.

Chapter Three

The next day, Hans was up a ladder nailing some honeysuckle against the porch when he heard the miller's voice calling to him from the road. He jumped off the ladder at once and ran down the garden. When he looked over the wall, he saw the miller with a large sack of flour on his back.

'Dear Hans,' said the miller, 'could you carry this sack of flour to the market for me?'

'I am so sorry,' said Hans, 'but I am really very busy today. I have to finish nailing up my honeysuckle, water all my flowers and mow my lawn.'

'I think that as I am going to give you my wheelbarrow, it is rather unfriendly of you to say no,' said the miller.

'Oh! I don't want to be unfriendly,' cried Hans. He ran inside for his cap and trudged off with the miller's big sack of flour on his shoulders.

It was a hot day and the road was very dusty. Hans had to sit down and rest many times, but he carried on and at last he reached the market. After he had waited there a while, he sold the sack of flour for a very good price, then returned home with the miller's money.

Early the next morning, the miller visited Hans to collect the money for his sack of flour, but Hans was so tired that he was still in bed.

'You are very lazy,' said the miller. 'As I am going to give you my wheelbarrow, you could work harder. I certainly don't like any of my friends to be lazy. I hope you don't mind me telling you? Good friends tell each other when they are in the wrong.'

'I am sorry,' said Hans, rubbing his eyes, 'but I was so tired that I thought I would lie in bed for a little bit and listen to the birds singing. Do you know that I always work better after hearing the birds sing?'

'I am glad to hear that,' said the

miller, clapping Hans on the back, 'as I want you to come up to the mill as soon as you are dressed and mend my barn roof for me.'

Poor Hans needed to get back to work in his garden as his flowers had not been watered for two days, but he did not like to say no to the miller, who was such a good friend to him.

'Do you think it would be unfriendly of me if I said I couldn't help you because I was busy?' Hans asked shyly.

'I do not think it is much to ask – I am going to give you my wheelbarrow! But if you refuse, I will go and do it myself,' replied the miller.

'Please don't,' cried Hans, who quickly got dressed and went up to the barn.

Hans worked on the barn roof all day long. At the end of the day, the miller came to see how he was getting on.

'Have you mended the hole in the roof yet, Hans?' cried the miller cheerfully.

'Yes, I've repaired it,' replied Hans, coming down the ladder.

'There is no better work than

the work one does for others,' said the miller. 'Go home and rest, as I want you to take my sheep to the mountain tomorrow.'

Poor Hans was afraid to say no. Early the next morning, the miller brought his sheep round to Hans's cottage, and Hans took them to the mountain. It took him the whole day to get there and back.

When he returned, he was so tired that he fell asleep in his chair and did not wake up until the next day.

The miller kept coming round and sending Hans off on long errands or getting him to help at the mill, and so Hans was never able to look after his flowers.

Hans was quite upset at times, afraid his flowers would think he had forgotten them, but he told himself that he was helping his best friend, the miller. After all, the miller had promised to give Hans his wheelbarrow, and he said all kinds of beautiful things about their friendship.

Chapter Four

One evening Hans was sitting by his fireside when a loud knock came at the door. It was a wild night and the wind was blowing and roaring around the house. Hans thought the knock must be coming from a poor traveller and he ran to open the door.

The miller was stood at his door, with a lantern in one hand and a big stick in the other.

'Dear Hans,' cried the miller, 'I am in trouble! My little boy has fallen off a ladder and hurt himself, and he needs the doctor. But the doctor lives so far away and it is such a bad night that it would be better if you went instead of me.

You know I am going to give you my wheelbarrow, and so it is only fair that you should do something for me in return.'

'Of course I will,' cried Hans. 'I will go at once. Please can you lend me your lantern? It's so dark I might fall into a ditch.'

'I am sorry, I can't,' replied the miller. 'It is my new lantern, and I would not like anything to happen to it.'

'Never mind, I will go without it,' said Hans. He put on his warm coat, tied a scarf around his neck, and set off.

It was a fierce storm that night. The night was so black that Hans could hardly see and the wind was so strong that he could hardly stand, but he was very brave and he carried on despite the conditions. After he had been walking for about three hours, he arrived at the doctor's house.

The doctor fetched his horse and lantern and rode off towards the miller's house, with Hans trudging behind him. The storm grew worse and the rain lashed down.

Hans could not see where he was going. After a while, he lost his way and wandered off onto the

moor, which was a very dangerous place as it was full of deep holes.

Poor Hans fell down one of the holes and died.

Everybody in the village went to Hans's funeral as everyone was very fond of him. Of course, the miller was there too.

'As I was his best friend,' said the miller, 'it is only fair that I should have the best place.' So the miller walked at the head of the procession in a long black cloak, and every now and then he wiped his eyes with a big pocket handkerchief.

'Everyone will miss Hans,' said

procession
A group of people moving forward in a line.

one of the villagers when the funeral service was over and they were all drinking hot tea and eating sweet cakes in the inn.

'It is a big loss to me, as I was about to give him my wheelbarrow,' said the miller. 'Now I don't know what to do with it. It is in the way at home, and it is so broken that no one would want to buy it. I will not give anything away again. One always suffers for being generous.'

'And that's the end of my story,' concluded Green Linnet.

'But what happened to the miller?' asked Water Rat.

'I don't know and I don't really care,' replied Green Linnet.

'It is clear that you don't care,' said Water Rat.

'Do you not see the message of the story?' asked Green Linnet.

'Hans does good things, and the miller talks about doing good things but never does them. Which do you think is the kinder way to behave? Who do you think is the kinder friend?'

'I think you should have told me the story had a message before you began. Then I would have listened for it!' said Water Rat. He whipped his tail round and disappeared back into his hole.

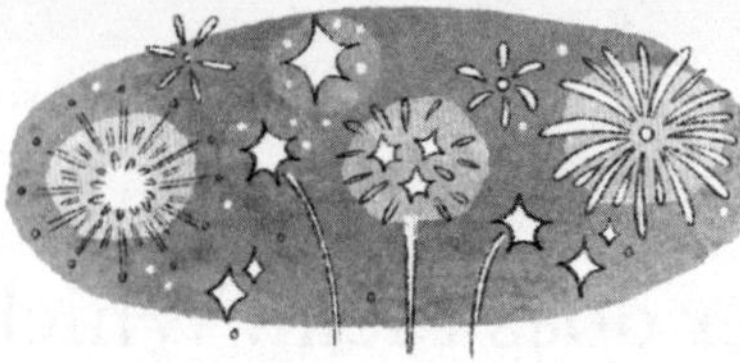

The Remarkable Rocket

Chapter One

The king's son was getting married and lots of celebrations were planned. On the big day, the prince and princess walked hand in hand under a canopy of purple velvet

sewn with little pearls. Then the bride and groom sat at the top of a long table in the Great Hall for a huge banquet, which lasted for five hours. After the banquet there was a ball, where the prince and princess danced in front of everyone and the king played the flute. He played very badly but no one ever dared to tell him this because he was the king.

The last of the celebrations was to be a grand fireworks display, which would start at exactly midnight. A large stand was set up for the fireworks at the end of the king's garden. The royal pyrotechnist was in charge of the fireworks. Early in the evening, she made sure that all of the fireworks were ready and in the correct place, then returned to the celebrations. As she left, there was a sharp, dry cough at the end of the garden.

'Ahem! Ahem!'

pyrotechnist
A person who makes fireworks.

It came from a tall, proud rocket, who was tied to the end of a long stick. He always coughed before he said anything, to attract attention. As soon as there was silence, the rocket coughed a third time and began his speech. He spoke with a slow, clear voice.

'It is so lucky for the king's son,' he began, 'that he is to be married on the very day on which I am to be let off.'

'I thought it was the other way round – that we were to be let off in the prince's honour,' said a little fountain shyly.

'That may be the reason for you,' the rocket replied, 'but with me it is different. I am a very remarkable rocket, and come from remarkable parents. My mother was the most famous Catherine wheel of her day, and was known for her graceful dancing. She spun round nineteen times before she went out and each time she spun round, she threw seven pink stars into the air. My father was a rocket like myself, from France. He flew so high that people were afraid he would never come down again. He did, though, and he made the most brilliant display of a shower of golden rain. The newspapers all wrote about his performance.'

At this point of the rocket's story, a sparkler interrupted to ask what the newspapers had said.

But the rocket couldn't remember exactly, and ignored the question.

'What was I saying?' he continued. 'I was talking about an interesting topic when I was so rudely interrupted.'

'You were talking about yourself,' whispered the Roman candle.

A cracker nearly exploded with laughter.

'What are you laughing at?' asked the rocket.

'I am laughing because I am happy,' replied the cracker.

'That is very selfish,' said the rocket angrily. 'Why should you be happy? You should be thinking about others. In fact, you should be thinking about me. I am always thinking about me, and I expect everybody else to do the same. If anything happened to me tonight, there would be no spectacular end to the fireworks. The prince and princess would never be happy again and the king would not get over it. It makes me cry to think of how important I am to this evening.'

'If you want to give joy to others tonight,' said the Roman candle, 'you had better keep yourself dry, or you won't go off!'

'None of you have a heart. Here you are laughing and joking and forgetting what a special day it is today, with the marriage of the prince and princess.'

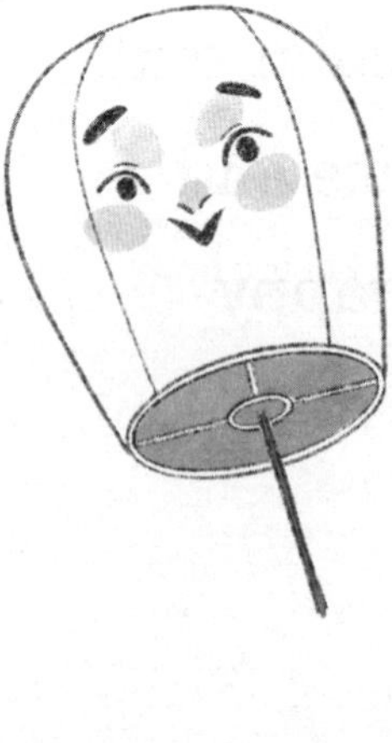

'I know it is a glorious day. When I fly up into the air, I will tell all the stars about it and you will see them twinkle,' said a small fire balloon.

'What a silly thing to say!' said the rocket. 'There is nothing inside you – you are hollow and empty. None of you can understand my friendship with the prince.'

'You don't even know him,' growled the Roman candle.

'I never said I knew him,' replied the rocket, who was beginning to feel tearful.

'You must keep yourself dry,' said the fire balloon. 'That is the most important thing.'

‘Important for you,’ answered the rocket, ‘but I shall cry if I choose to!’ He burst into tears, which flowed down his stick like raindrops.

‘He is crying when there is nothing to cry about!’ said a Catherine wheel.

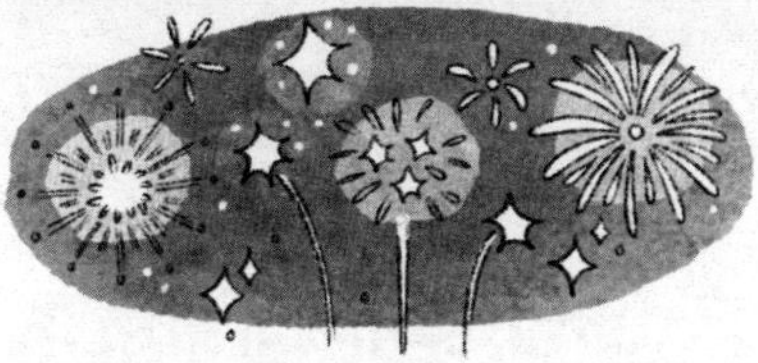

Chapter Two

The moon rose in the sky like a shiny, silver shield, the stars began to shine, and music came from the palace. The prince and princess were leading a dance.

The clock chimed at ten o'clock, then eleven, and finally twelve. At the stroke of midnight, everyone came out onto the terrace, and the king sent for the royal pyrotechnist.

'Let the fireworks begin!' cried the king to everyone gathered.

The fireworks started. It was a magnificent display.

Whizz! went the Catherine wheel, as she spun round and round.

Boom! went the Roman candle.

Then the fountains danced, and the sparklers made everything look silver.

'Goodbye,' cried the fire balloon as he soared away, dropping tiny blue sparks as he went.

Bang! answered the crackers, who were having so much fun.

Every firework was a great success, except for the remarkable rocket. He was so damp from crying that when his big moment came, he could not go off at all.

The next day, the workmen came to tidy everything away. They did not notice the rocket until they were just about to leave. Then one of them caught sight of him.

'What a bad firework!' the worker said, and he threw the rocket over the palace wall into a ditch. The rocket did not find it comfortable in the muddy ditch and felt very sorry for himself.

A little frog with bright eyes and a green patchy coat swam up to the rocket, smiling widely.

'I see someone new has arrived!' said the frog. 'Do you think it will rain this afternoon? I hope so. I love being muddy and wet!'

'Ahem! Ahem!' said the rocket, beginning to cough.

‘What a splendid voice you have!’ cried the frog. ‘Although croaking is the most musical sound to me. You will hear me and my friends singing this evening.’

‘Ahem!’ said the rocket angrily.

He was annoyed that he could not get a word in.

'I hope you will listen to us this evening. I am off to look for my children – I am afraid the pike may eat them. Well, goodbye. I have enjoyed our chat,' said the frog.

‘Chat, indeed!’ said the rocket crossly. ‘You have talked the whole time. That is not a chat.’

‘Somebody must listen,’ replied the frog, ‘and I like to do all the talking. It saves time and stops arguments.’

‘But I like arguments,’ said the rocket crossly.

‘Well, I don’t like arguments.’ said the frog. ‘Goodbye for a second time. I see my children in the distance.’ The little frog swam away.

'People who talk about themselves are selfish. I will go back to the palace soon as I am loved

by everyone there. The prince and princess were married yesterday in my honour. Of course, you know nothing about this as you live out here, far from anywhere,' rambled the rocket.

'It's no good talking to the frog – he's gone!' a dragonfly told the rocket. The dragonfly was sitting on top of a large brown bulrush.

'That is his loss, not mine,'

answered the rocket. 'I am not going to stop talking to him just because he is not listening. I like hearing myself talk.'

The dragonfly did not want to stay and listen to the rocket talking all about himself, so he spread out his delicate wings and soared into the sky, leaving the rocket to sink further into the mud.

Chapter Three

After some time, a large duck swam up to the rocket.

'Quack, quack, quack,' she said. 'What a strange shape you are! May I ask what you do?'

'You may be surprised to hear that I can fly up into the sky and come down in a shower of sparkling golden rain.'

'I don't think much of that,' said the duck. 'What use is that to anyone? If you could plough the fields like the ox, or pull a cart like the horse, or look after the sheep like the collie dog, that would be something.'

'My good creature,' cried the rocket, 'a person as important as me is never useful. We have special talents.'

'Well,' said the duck, who was a very peaceful person and never quarrelled with anyone, 'everybody has different strengths. Are you going to live here?'

'Oh, absolutely not!' cried the rocket. 'I am only visiting. I find this place rather drab and will be going back to the palace soon. I am going to be something magnificent in the world.'

'Very good!' said the duck, and she swam away.

'I am glad she has gone. Her mind is not as grand as mine,' the rocket said to himself as he sank a little deeper into the mud.

He was thinking of how being so clever was lonely, when suddenly two little boys ran down the bank with a kettle and handfuls of twigs.

This must be my moment! Someone from the palace has come to fetch me, thought the rocket.

'Look at this old stick!' cried one of the boys. 'I wonder how it got down here?'

The boy picked the rocket out of the ditch.

'Did he say *old* stick?' muttered the rocket. 'That's impossible. He must have said *gold* stick.'

'Let's use the old stick on our fire!'

said the other boy. 'It will make a bigger fire and boil our kettle quicker.'

The boys made a pile of twigs and put the rocket on top of it. Then they lit the fire and put the kettle on it.

'This is magnificent!' exclaimed the rocket. 'They are going to let me off in the daytime, so everyone will see me.'

The boys lay down and closed their eyes to have a quick nap whilst they waited for the kettle to boil.

The rocket was very damp, so he took a long time to burn. At last, however, the fire caught him.

'Now I am going off!' he cried. He made himself very stiff and straight. 'I will fly higher than the stars, higher than the moon, and even higher than the sun! In fact, I shall go so high that …'

Fizz! Fizz! Fizz!

He went straight up into the air!

'Wonderful!' he cried. 'I am such a success!'

But nobody saw the rocket.

He felt a strange tingling feeling all over.

'Now I am going to explode,' he cried. 'I will set the whole world on fire, and make such a noise that nobody will talk about anything else for a whole year!'

He certainly did explode. *Bang! Bang! Bang!*

But nobody heard the rocket, not even the two boys, who were fast asleep.

Then all that was left of him was the stick, which fell down, back into the ditch.

Oscar Wilde

Oscar Wilde was born in Dublin in 1854. He later moved to London where he published a range of poems, plays and fairy tales. Wilde's personal life was colourful but tragic. He was gay in a time when it was illegal, and he went to prison for it. Today he is one of the most quoted writers. One of his most famous quotes is: 'Be yourself; everyone else is already taken'.